THE LOUD HOUSE

#12 "THE CASE OF THE STOLEN DRAWERS"

PAPERCUTZ
New York

#12 "THE CASE OF THE STOLEN DRAWERS"

The Case of the Stolen Drawers **10**

Going Coco-Nuts! **16**

Ollie Ollie Oxen Free **20**

Tongue Tied **25**

Zach and the Mean Chalk **31**

Comic Relief **36**

Level Up **41**

Meat Your Maker **45**

Model Pets **49**

Diagnosis: Loud **54**

Cakenstein's Monsters **57**

Preview of THE LOUD HOUSE
SUMMER SPECIAL
"Lucy's Summer Fashion Tips" **60**

Preview of THE
CASAGRANDES SPECIAL
"The Great Escape" **62**

"THE CASE OF THE STOLEN DRAWERS"
Kiernan Sjursen-Lien — Writer
Tyler Koberstein — Artist, Colorist
Wilson Ramos Jr. — Letterer

"MEAT YOUR MAKER"
Derek Fridolfs — Writer
George Holguin — Artist
Vic Miyuki — Colorist
Wilson Ramos Jr. — Letterer

"GOING COCO-NUTS!"
Jair Holguin — Writer
Erin Hunting — Artist, Colorist
Wilson Ramos Jr. — Letterer

"MODEL PETS"
Kacey Wooley-Huang — Writer
Kelsey Wooley — Artist, Colorist
Wilson Ramos Jr. — Letterer

"OLLIE OLLIE OXEN FREE"
Jair Holguin — Writer
Zazo Aguiar — Artist, Colorist
Vic Miyuki — Colorist
Wilson Ramos Jr. — Letterer

"DIAGNOSIS: LOUD"
Paul Allor — Writer
Melissa Kleynowski — Artist
Princess Bizares — Colorist
Wilson Ramos Jr. — Letterer

"TONGUE TIED"
Julia Guillen — Writer
Ron Bradley — Artist, Colorist
Wilson Ramos Jr. — Letterer

"CAKENSTEIN'S MONSTER"
Paul Allor — Writer
Erin Hunting — Artist, Colorist
Wilson Ramos Jr. — Letterer

"ZACH AND THE MEAN CHALK"
Derek Fridolfs — Writer
Erin Hyde — Artist, Colorist
Wilson Ramos Jr. — Letterer

"LUCY'S SUMMER FASHION TIPS" from THE LOUD HOUSE SUMMER SPECIAL
Caitlin Fein — Writer
Max Alley — Artist
Peter Bertucci — Colorist
Wilson Ramos Jr. — Letterer

"COMIC RELIEF"
Caitlin Fein — Writer
Zazo Aguiar — Artist,
Vic Miyuki — Colorist
Wilson Ramos Jr. — Letterer

"THE GREAT ESCAPE" from THE CASA-GRANDES SPECIAL "WE'RE ALL FAMILIA"
Derek Fridolfs — Writer
Suzannah Rowntree — Penciler
Zazo Aguiar — Inker, Colorist
Wilson Ramos Jr. — Letterer

"LEVEL UP"
Kiernan Sjursen-Lien — Writer
Lee-Roy Lahey — Artist
Peter Bertucci — Colorist
Wilson Ramos Jr. — Letterer

TODD OMAN — Cover Artist

JORDAN ROSATO — Endpapers
JAMES SALERNO — Sr. Art Director/Nickelodeon
JAYJAY JACKSON — Design
EMMA BONE, CAITLIN FEIN, KRISTEN G. SMITH, NEIL WADE, DANA CLUVERIUS, MOLLIE FREILICH — Special Thanks
JEFF WHITMAN — Editor
JOAN HILTY — Editor/Nickelodeon
JIM SALICRUP
Editor-in-Chief

ISBN: 978-1-5458-0621-0 paperback edition
ISBN: 978-1-5458-0620-3 hardcover edition

Papercutz books may be purchased for business or promotional use. For information on bulk purchases please contact Macmillan Corporate and Premium Sales Department at (800) 221-7945 x5442.

Printed in China
March 2021

Distributed by Macmillan
First Printing

MEET THE LOUD FAMILY
and friends!

LINCOLN LOUD
THE MIDDLE CHILD

Lincoln is the middle child, with five older sisters and five younger sisters. He has learned that surviving the Loud household means staying a step ahead. He's the man with a plan, always coming up with a way to get what he wants or deal with a problem, even if things inevitably go wrong. Being the only boy comes with some perks. Lincoln gets his own room – even if it's just a converted linen closet. On the other hand, being the only boy also means he sometimes gets a little too much attention from his sisters. They mother him, tease him, and use him as the occasional lab rat or fashion show participant. Lincoln's sisters may drive him crazy, but he loves them and is always willing to help out if they need him.

LORI LOUD
THE OLDEST

As the first-born child of the Loud Clan, Lori sees herself as the boss of all her siblings. She feels she's paved the way for them and deserves extra respect. Her signature traits are rolling her eyes, texting her boyfriend, Bobby, and literally saying "literally" all the time. Because she's the oldest and most experienced sibling, Lori can be a great ally, so it pays to stay on her good side, especially since she can drive.

LENI LOUD
THE FASHIONISTA

Leni spends most of her time designing outfits and accessorizing. She always falls for Luan's pranks, and sometimes walks into walls when she's talking (she's not great at doing two things at once). Leni might be flighty, but she's the sweetest of the Loud siblings and truly has a heart of gold (even though she's pretty sure it's a heart of blood).

LUNA LOUD
THE ROCK STAR

Luna is loud, boisterous, freewheeling, and her energy is always cranked to 11. She thinks about music so much that she even talks in song lyrics. On the off-chance she doesn't have her guitar with her, everything can and will be turned into a musical instrument. You can always count on Luna to help out, and she'll do most anything you ask, as long as you're okay with her supplying a rocking guitar accompaniment.

MR COCONUTS

Luan Loud's wise-cracking dummy.

LUAN LOUD
THE JOKESTER

Luan's a standup comedienne who provides a nonstop barrage of silly puns. She's big on prop comedy too – squirting flowers and whoopee cushions – so you have to be on your toes whenever she's around. She loves to pull pranks and is a really good ventriloquist – she is often found doing bits with her dummy, Mr. Coconuts. Luan never lets anything get her down; to her, laughter IS the best medicine.

BITEY

FANGS

LYNN LOUD
THE ATHLETE

Lynn is athletic and full of energy and is always looking for a teammate. With her, it's all sports all the time. She'll turn anything into a sport. Putting away eggs? Jump shot! Score! Cleaning up the eggs? Slap shot! Score! Lynn is very competitive, but despite her competitive nature, she always tries to just have a good time.

LUCY LOUD
THE EMO

You can always count on Lucy to give the morbid point of view in any given situation. She is obsessed with all things spooky and dark – funerals, vampires, séances, and the like. She wears mostly black and writes moody poetry. She's usually quiet and keeps to herself. Lucy has a way of mysteriously appearing out of nowhere, and try as they might, her siblings never get used to this.

LOLA LOUD
THE BEAUTY QUEEN)

Lola could not be more different from her twin sister, Lana. She's a pageant powerhouse whose interests include glitter, photo shoots, and her own beautiful, beautiful face. But don't let her cute, gap-toothed smile fool you; underneath all the sugar and spice lurks a Machiavellian mastermind. Whatever Lola wants, Lola gets – or else. She's the eyes and ears of the household and never resists an opportunity to tattle on troublemakers. But if you stay on Lola's good side, you've got yourself a fierce ally – and a lifetime supply of free makeovers.

LANA LOUD
THE TOMBOY

Lana is the rough-and-tumble sparkplug counterpart to her twin sister, Lola. She's all about reptiles, mud pies, and muffler repair. She's the resident Ms. Fix-it and is always ready to lend a hand – the dirtier the job, the better. Need your toilet unclogged? Snake fed? Back-zit popped? Lana's your gal. All she asks in return is a little A-B-C gum, or a handful of kibble (she often sneaks it from the dog bowl).

LISA LOUD
THE GENIUS

Lisa is smarter than the rest of her siblings combined. She'll most likely be a rocket scientist, or a brain surgeon, or an evil genius who takes over the world. Lisa spends most of her time working in her lab (the family has gotten used to the explosions), and says her research leaves little time for frivolous human pursuits like "playing" or "getting haircuts." That said, she's always there to help with a homework question, or to explain why the sky is blue, or to point out the structural flaws in someone's pillow fort. Lisa says it's the least she can do for her favorite test subjects, er, siblings.

LILY LOUD
THE BABY

Lily is a giggly, drooly, diaper-ditching free spirit, affectionately known as "the poop machine." You can't keep a nappy on this kid – she's like a teething Houdini. But even when Lily's running wild, dropping rancid diaper bombs, or drooling all over the remote, she always brings a smile to everyone's face (and a clothespin to their nose). Lily is everyone's favorite little buddy, and the whole family loves her unconditionally.

POP POP

Albert, the Loud kids' grandfather, currently lives at Sunset Canyon Retirement Community after dedicating his life to working in the military. Pop Pop spends his days dominating at shuffleboard, eating pudding, and going on adventures with his pals Bernie, Scoots, and Seymour and his girlfriend, Myrtle. Pop Pop is upbeat, fun-loving, and cherishes spending time with his grandchildren.

CHARLES

WALT

CLIFF

GEO

RITA LOUD

Mother to the eleven Loud kids, Mom (Rita Loud) wears many different hats. She's a chauffeur, homework-checker, and barf-cleaner-upper all rolled into one. She's always there for her kids and ready to jump into action during a crisis, whether it's a fight between the twins or Leni's missing shoe. When she's not chasing the kids around or at her day job as a dental hygienist, Mom pursues her passion: writing. She also loves taking on house projects and is very handy with tools (guess that's where Lana gets it from). Between writing, working, and being a mom, her days are always hectic but she wouldn't have it any other way.

LYNN LOUD SR.

Dad (Lynn Loud Sr.) is a fun-loving, upbeat aspiring chef. A kid-at-heart, he's not above taking part in the kids' zany schemes. In addition to cooking, Dad loves his van, playing the cowbell. and making puns. Before meeting Mom, Dad spent a semester in England and has been obsessed with British culture ever since – and sometimes "accidentally" slips into a British accent. When Dad's not wrangling the kids, he's pursuing his dream of opening his own restaurant where he hopes to make his "Lynn-sagnas" world-famous.

CLYDE McBRIDE
THE BEST FRIEND

Clyde is Lincoln's partner in crime. He's always willing to go along with Lincoln's crazy schemes (even if he sees the flaws in them up-front). Lincoln and Clyde are two peas in a pod and share pretty much all of the same tastes in movies, comics, TV shows, toys — you name it. As an only child, Clyde envies Lincoln — how cool would it be to always have siblings around to talk to? But since Clyde spends so much time at the Loud household, he's almost an honorary sibling anyway.

ZACH GURDLE

Zach is a self-admitted nerd who's obsessed with aliens and conspiracy theories. He lives between a freeway and a circus, so the chaos of the Loud House doesn't faze him. He and Rusty occasionally butt heads, but deep down, it's all love.

RUSTY SPOKES

Rusty is a self-proclaimed ladies' man who's always the first to dish out girl advice — even though he's never been on an actual date. His dad owns a suit rental service, so occasionally Rusty can hook the gang up with some dapper duds — just as long as no one gets anything dirty.

LIAM

Liam is an enthusiastic, sweet-natured farm boy full of down-home wisdom. He loves hanging out with his Mee Maw, wrestling his prize pig Virginia, and sharing his farm-to-table produce with the rest of the gang.

STELLA

Stella Zhau is a quirky, carefree girl who's new to Royal Woods. She has tons of interests, like trying on wigs, playing laser tag, eating curly fries, and hanging with her friends. But what she loves the most is tech — she always wants to dismantle electronics and put them back together again.

MR. BUD GROUSE

Mr. Grouse is the Louds's next-door-neighbor. The Louds often go to him for favors which he normally rejects – unless there's a chance for him to score one of Dad's famous Lynn-sagnas. Mr. Grouse loves gardening, relaxing in his recliner, and keeping anything of the Louds's that flies into his yard (his catchphrase, after all, is "my yard, my property!").

RONNIE ANNE SANTIAGO

Ronnie Anne's a skateboarding city girl now. She's fearless, free-spirited, and always quick to come up with a plan. She's one tough cookie, but she also has a sweet side. Ronnie Anne loves helping her family, and that's taught her to help others, too. When she's not pitching in at the family mercado, you can find her exploring the neighborhood with her best friend Sid, or ordering hot dogs with her skater buds Casey, Nikki, and Sameer.

BOBBY SANTIAGO

Bobby is Ronnie Anne's big bro. He's a student and one of the hardest workers in the city! He loves his family and loves working at the Mercado. As his Abuelo's right hand man, Bobby can't wait to take over the family business one day. He's a big kid at heart, and his clumsiness gets him into some sticky situations at work, like locking himself in the freezer. Mercado mishaps aside, everyone in the neighborhood loves to come to the store and talk to Bobby.

SERGIO

Sergio is the Casagrandes' beloved pet parrot. He's a blunt, sassy bird who "thinks" he's full of wisdom, and always has something to say. The Casagrandes have to keep a close eye on their credit card as Sergio is addicted to online shopping and is always asking the family to buy him some new gadget he saw on TV. Sergio is most loyal to Rosa and serves as her wing-man, partner in crime, taste tester, and confidant. Sergio is quite popular in the neighborhood and is always up for a good time.

VITO FILLIPONIO

Vito is one of Rosa and Hector's oldest and dearest friends, and a frequent customer at the Mercado. He's lovable, nosy, and usually overstays his welcome, but there is nothing he wouldn't do for his loved ones and his dogs, Big Tony and Little Sal.

HECTOR CASAGRANDE

Hector is Carlos and Maria's dad, and the Abuelo of the family (that means grandpa)! He owns the Mercado on the ground floor of their apartment building and takes great pride in his work, his family, and being the unofficial "mayor" of the block. He loves to tell stories, share his ideas, and gossip (even though he won't admit it). You can find him working in the Mercado, playing guitar, or watching his favorite telenovela.

ROSA CASAGRANDE

Rosa is Carlos and Maria's mom and the Abuela of the family (that means grandma)! She's the head of the household, the wisest Casagrande, and the master cook with a superhuman ability to tell when anyone in the house is hungry. She often tries to fix problems or illnesses with traditional Mexican home remedies and potions. She's very protective of her family... sometimes a little too much.

15

17

21

22

23

"TONGUE-TIED"

29

"ZACH AND THE MEAN CHALK"

32

34

"COMIC RELIEF"

40

"LEVEL UP"

44

"MEAT YOUR MAKER"

48

"MODEL PETS"

53

56

58

Be sure to pick up THE LOUD HOUSE SUMMER SPECIAL available wherever books are sold, coming this summer!

"THE GREAT ESCAPE"

Be sure to pick up THE CASAGRANDES SPECIAL "We're All Familia" available soon wherever books are sold!

WATCH OUT FOR PAPERCUTZ™

Welcome to the tantalizing twelfth THE LOUD HOUSE graphic novel "The Case of the Stolen Drawers," from Papercutz, those well-attired types dedicated to publishing great graphic novels for all ages. I'm Jim Salicrup, Editor-in-Chief and part-time gag writer for Luan Loud. One of the best "problems" any publisher can have is people complaining that you don't come out with enough books featuring their favorite characters. At Papercutz, we're bombarded by requests for more of THE LOUD HOUSE graphic novels. So, we heard you, and we listened, and we're happy to announce the following special Papercutz graphic novels.

First off, there's THE LOUD HOUSE SUMMER SPECIAL. Summer truly is special. School's out and there's plenty of time for fun. Not that that Loud family don't have fun all year 'round, but if you live somewhere where it snows in the winter, those hot summer beach days are precious. So, Lincoln and his sisters Lori, Leni, Luna, Lynn, Luan, Lucy (yes, even Lucy!), Lola, Lana, and Lily can't wait to hit the beach or chill out by the pool, or just look for a delicious icy treat to beat the heat. The Casagrandes are included in the fun as well. Ronnie Anne, Bobby, and the rest of their extended family are searching for foolproof ways of handling the scorching summer in the big city. This extra-special graphic novel features a mix of new stories and past favorites from THE LOUD HOUSE graphic novel series.

And speaking of THE CASAGRANDES, guess who are starring in a special graphic novel all of their own? That's right! Papercutz presents the very first THE CASAGRANDES graphic novel. When Lincoln Loud's good friend Ronnie Anne, and Lori's boyfriend (Ronnie Anne's brother) Bobby, and their mother, Maria, moved away from Royal Oaks to an apartment in the Big City, above their abuelo's (grandpaprents) mercado, it was a big change. Now they're with the kid's abuelos, Hector and Rosa, as well as Rosa's brother, Carlos, his wife, Frida, and their four kids, Carlota, CJ (Carlos Jr.), Carl, and Carlitos, not to mention their pets, Lalo (the dog) and Sergio (the bird). Likewise, this graphic novel features new stories and past favorites which appeared in THE LOUD HOUSE graphic novels.

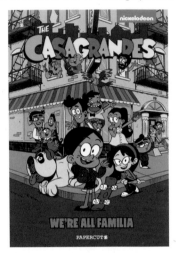

We've even included a preview story from each SPECIAL in this very graphic novel — so check it out! And if those two graphic novels, plus the shows themselves on Nickelodeon, can't satisfy your cravings for more of THE LOUD HOUSE, don't worry. Coming soon is the all-new THE LOUD HOUSE #13 "Lucy Rolls the Dice"! Find out what happens when a storm knocks out the electricity at the Loud house and the kids have to find new ways to entertain themselves. With these eleven kids, we're sure they'll come up with a few surprises.

Thanks,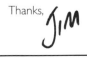

STAY IN TOUCH!

EMAIL: salicrup@papercutz.com
WEB: papercutz.com
TWITTER: @papercutzgn
INSTAGRAM: @papercutzgn
FACEBOOK: PAPERCUTZGRAPHICNOVELS
FANMAIL: Papercutz, 160 Broadway, Suite 700, East Wing, New York, NY 10038

Go to papercutz.com and sign up for the free Papercutz e-newsletter!